Balboa Press books may be ordered through booksellers or by contacting:

Balboa Press
A Division of Hay House
1663 Liberty Drive
Bloomington, IN 47403
www.balboapress.com
844-682-1282

ISBN: 979-8-7652-3164-7 (sc)
ISBN: 979-8-7652-3232-3 (e)

Library of Congress Control Number: 2022914136

Print information available on the last page.

Balboa Press rev. date: 01/17/2023

BALBOA.PRESS

Mable

Mable

Mable Mable big and able, get your elbows off the table!

Mable Mable so tall
and true, don't burp at
the table. It's rude!

Mable Mable my beautiful rose, get your fingers out of your nose!

Mable Mable my darling baby girl, your hair is so beautiful, without all that food in your curls.

Mable Mable so fine and so fair, please don't slouch, you must sit up in your chair.

Mable Mable be a
winner, please sit down
and eat your dinner!

Mable Mable you're so big,
please don't eat like a pig

Mable Mable my sweet, sweet apple pie, please don't poke your brother in the eye

Mable Mable it may sound like I'm picking on you, but I assure you this is not true!

Mable Mable don't be blue, I'm not saying this to be rude, I'm really helping because I love you!

Printed in the United States
by Baker & Taylor Publisher Services